Hands-On Science Fun

How to Make ICE CREAM in a BAG

A 4D Book

by Barbara Alpert

PEBBLE
a capstone imprint

Pebble Plus is published by Capstone Press,
1710 Roe Crest Drive, North Mankato, Minnesota 56003
www.mycapstone.com

Copyright © 2019 by Capstone Press, a Capstone imprint. All rights reserved. No part of this publication may be reproduced in whole or in part, or stored in a retrieval system, or transmitted in any form or by any means, electronic, mechanical, photocopying, recording, or otherwise, without written permission of the publisher.

Library of Congress Cataloging-in-Publication Data
is available on the Library of Congress website.

ISBN 978-1-9771-0226-3 (library binding)
ISBN 978-1-9771-0517-2 (paperback)
ISBN 978-1-9771-0230-0 (ebook pdf)

Editorial Credits
Carrie Braulick Sheely, editor; Sarah Bennett, designer; Marcy Morin, scheduler and project producer; Sarah Schuette, photo stylist and project producer; Katy LaVigne, production specialist

Photo Credits
All photographs by Capstone Studio/Karon Dubke except for: Shutterstock/Serhiy Smirnov, cover (thermometer icon)

Note to Parents and Teachers

The Hands-On Science Fun set supports national science standards related to physical science. This book describes and illustrates making ice cream in a bag. The images support early readers in understanding the text. The repetition of words and phrases helps early readers learn new words. This book also introduces early readers to subject-specific vocabulary words, which are defined in the Glossary section. Early readers may need assistance to read some words and to use the Table of Contents, Glossary, Read More, Internet Sites, Critical Thinking Questions, and Index sections of the book.

1. Ask an adult to download the app.   **Capstone 4D** Education
2. Scan the pages with the star.
3. Enjoy your cool stuff!

OR

Use this password at capstone4D.com

icecream02263

Printed and bound in China.
970

Table of Contents

Getting Started 4

Making Ice Cream in a Bag 6

How Does It Work? 16

    Glossary 22

    Read More 23

    Internet Sites 23

    Critical Thinking Questions 24

    Index 24

Safety Note:
Please ask an adult for help in making your ice cream.

Getting Started

Yum! On a hot day, ice cream is a great treat! You can make your own ice cream in a bag. Then let science tickle your taste buds!

Here's what you need:

 1 cup (240 mL) half-and-half

 1 sandwich-size zip-top bag

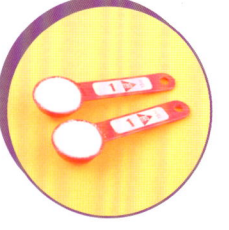 2 tablespoons (30 mL) sugar

 1 teaspoon (5 mL) vanilla

 3 cups (720 mL) ice cubes

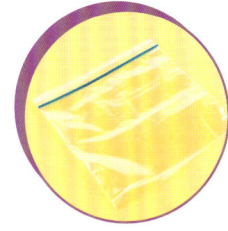 1 gallon-size zip-top bag

 1/3 cup (80 mL) kosher salt

 towel

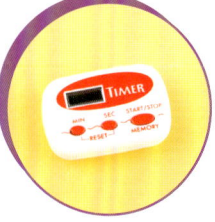 timer

 spoon

Making Ice Cream in a Bag

Pour half-and-half into the sandwich bag. Add the sugar and vanilla. Squeeze out the air. Seal the bag. You have your cream! Now let's ice it!

7

Put the ice into the gallon bag.
Pour salt into the bag
with the ice. Put the sandwich
bag into the gallon bag.
Seal the bag tight.

Wrap the bag in a towel.

Start the timer.

Shake the bag hard!

Keep shaking for six minutes.

Set the bag down to finish freezing. Wait five more minutes. Now grab your spoon! Eat the ice cream right out of the bag!

Next time, experiment! Will more salt freeze it faster? Add fruit or candy. Add about ¼ cup (60 mL) chocolate syrup. You are the chef-scientist! It's up to you!

How Does It Work?

Water turns to ice at its freezing point. That's 32 degrees Fahrenheit (0 degrees Celsius). It goes from liquid to solid.

liquid water

solid water (ice)

17

The cream mixture has more than water in it. It must get below water's freezing point to turn solid. The salt is the secret. Adding salt to the bag of ice cools the cream below freezing.

19

Shaking spreads the salt and melts the ice. Your ice cream cools evenly. It gets smooth. Shaking also adds air. This makes the ice cream light. Yum!

21

Glossary

freezing point—the temperature at which a liquid turns into a solid when cooled; water's freezing point is 32 degrees Fahrenheit (0 degrees Celsius), but salt lowers the freezing point

ice—frozen water

liquid—a wet substance that can be poured, such as water

melt—to change from a solid into a liquid

scientist—a person who studies the world around us

seal—to close something up

solid—a substance that holds its shape

taste bud—one of the small organs on the top of the tongue that tell people what things taste like

Read More

Dunne, Abbie. *Matter.* Physical Science. North Mankato, Minn.: Capstone, 2017.

Polinksy, Paige V. *Super Simple Experiments with Heat and Cold: Fun and Innovative Science Projects.* Super Simple Science at Work. Minneapolis: Abdo Publishing Company, 2017.

Rompella, Natalie. *Experiments in Material and Matter with Toys and Everyday Stuff.* Fun Science. North Mankato, Minn.: Capstone Press, 2016.

Internet Sites

Use FactHound to find Internet sites related to this book.

Visit *www.facthound.com*

Just type 9781977102263 and go.

Check out projects, games and lots more at
www.capstonekids.com

Critical Thinking Questions

1. What do you think would happen if you didn't shake the bag?

2. What do you think would happen if you added less salt to the bag?

3. The half-and-half liquid changed into a solid. The ice changed into a liquid. What other things can change in one of these ways?

Index

experimenting, 14
freezing point, 16, 18
half-and-half, 6
liquid, 16
salt, 8, 14, 18, 20
science, 4

shaking, 10, 20
solid, 16, 18
sugar, 6
vanilla, 6
water, 16, 18